This book belongs to:

_____

_____

_____

For Francey

First published 2017 by Walker Books Ltd,
87 Vauxhall Walk, London SE11 5HJ
This edition published 2018
2 4 6 8 10 9 7 5 3 1
© 2017 Yasmeen Ismail
The right of Yasmeen Ismail to be identified as author/illustrator of this work has been asserted
by her in accordance with the Copyright, Designs and Patents Act 1988
This book has been typeset in Bentham
Printed in China

British Library Cataloguing in Publication Data:
a catalogue record for this book is available from the British Library
ISBN 978-1-4063-8006-4
www.walker.co.uk

WALKER BOOKS
AND SUBSIDIARIES
LONDON • BOSTON • SYDNEY • AUCKLAND

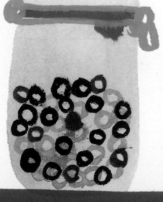

Kiki and Bobo woke up one morning.
"What day is it today?" said Kiki. "Is it
waffle day?"

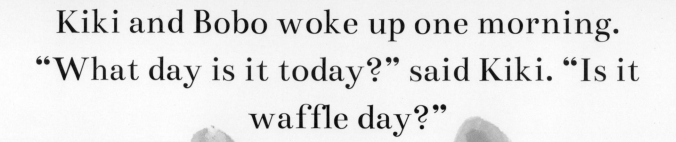

"No, Kiki," said Bobo. "Don't you know what day it is? It's far more special than waffle day."

"It's so special I've got lots to do. I'm going to the shops. Bye Kiki."

"What day can it be?" said Kiki.
"It must be Bobo's birthday. I'll surprise him
with a party. First I'll bake him a cake."

Bobo was busy at the shops.
He picked up tasty things to eat.
"Mmm, spaghetti," he said.
"Sausages and buns and
marshmallows too. Yummy!"

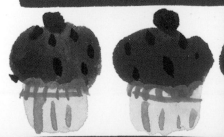

Kiki's cake was baking in the oven.
"I'll blow up balloons," she said. Puff!
Puff! Puff! "Bobo will like these."

Bobo went into the toy shop. "I want to buy something really special. That looks perfect," he said. He counted all his coins. "I have just enough."

Kiki was nearly ready.
"Bobo will be back soon," she said.
"I'd better put on my party dress."

On his way home Bobo picked some flowers.
"I'll give these to Kiki," he said.

Kiki had just finished putting up
the bunting when Bobo arrived.

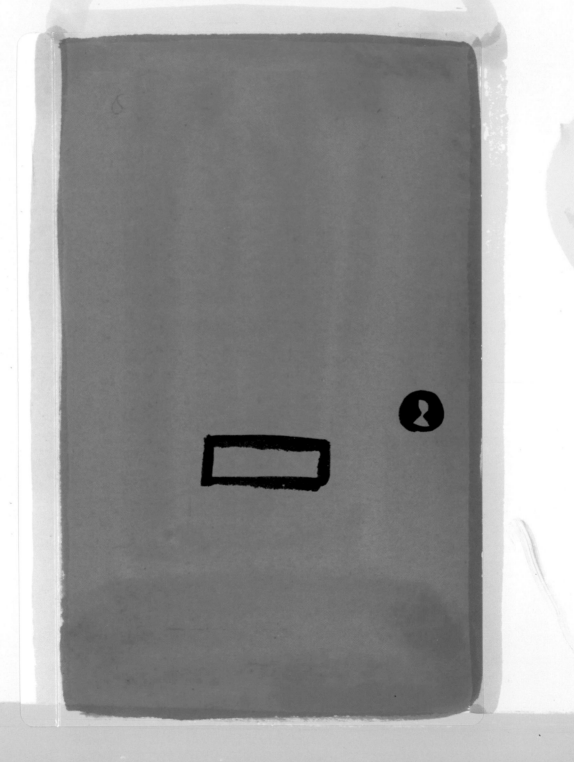

"No, Kiki," said Bobo. "It's YOUR birthday today! That's why today is a special day. Happy Birthday, Kiki!"

"It's MY birthday?" said Kiki.
"I've been so busy I'd forgotten!"

What a super
surprise for Kiki.

Kiki and Bobo celebrated Kiki's birthday
all day. They had cake and balloons
and marshmallows.

All their friends joined in and they had
a very lovely, very special day.
Hip Hip Hooray!

Also by Yasmeen Ismail:

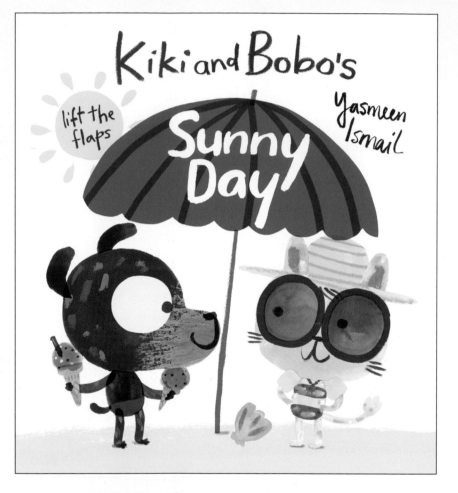

ISBN: 978-1-4063-7887-0